My Diary Notes(Articles)

Dr. Renuka. KP

Ukiyoto Publishing

All global publishing rights are held by

Ukiyoto Publishing

Published in 2024

Content Copyright © Dr. Renuka. KP

ISBN 9789364947053

All rights reserved.

No part of this publication may be reproduced, transmitted, or stored in a retrieval system, in any form by any means, electronic, mechanical, photocopying, recording or otherwise, without the prior permission of the publisher.

The moral rights of the author have been asserted.

This book is sold subject to the condition that it shall not by way of trade or otherwise, be lent, resold, hired out or otherwise circulated, without the publisher's prior consent, in any form of binding or cover other than that in which it is published.

www.ukiyoto.com

In fond memories of my demised parents and siblings

Contents

The Need for Value-based education for a Developed Nation	1
Happy Vijayadashami	6
The Relevance of Spirituality in Daily Life	8
Happy Diwali	13
Health Insurance for the Retirees-A Review	15
Sivarathri-Myth and Essence	19
The Need of Self-transformation Today	22
The Greatest Wealth is Health. How is it to be maintained?	26
The Social Media	32
It is Just a Dream	35
The Angels on Earth	40
About the Author	*42*

The Need for Value-based education for a Developed Nation

Healthy well-educated citizens are the backbone of every developed nation. As better basic education and good health play crucial roles in molding a child mentally and physically healthy, we should pay more attention to these two sectors because children are the foundation of a developed nation. This sheds light on the importance of education in bringing up a child with moral values from the beginning of growth and the necessity of always providing better facilities for keeping them healthy. Without a strong basement, the construction on it will not become strong.

Nowadays even if whatever academic qualifications we gather, most of us are seen as utter failures in real life. If we go through social media we can see the depth of weakness of our youth who are struggling to keep their relationships stable and maintain healthy social interactions with others. People are seen as weak in facing challenges and highly disturbed. Most people are seen as short-tempered without any mental power and are also under the grip of lifestyle diseases. Due to the absence of moral values and self-control, how many anti-social activities, divorces, and crimes are reported daily? Unfortunately, it is seen that most of the clients in all these crimes are academically qualified. This sheds light on the inadequacy of our academic syllabus and the standard of qualifications. It has turned out only as a way of getting a job for the students and a way of earnings for education providers. Nothing is done to develop their caliber to lead a successful life. So we have to think deeply about the quality of education and its management.

Education not only provides children to study how to read and write and obtain an academic qualification to get a job but also gives knowledge about ethics, empathy, critical thinking skills necessary for their successful life, and emotional stability. It should be an inner engineering for the students. As this is not available in the curriculum, some pupils are seen outside seeking motivators, gurus, etc. Several schools and educational institutions have incorporated moral education into their curriculum in a limited way. A value based Education helps children to understand their values and beliefs, right and wrong, empathy, and self-respect. It helps them to develop an understanding of different perspectives and learn to consider the feelings and needs of others, enabling them to make critical decisions by analyzing any situation.

Ethical principles help children recognize and avoid harmful habits such as addiction to drugs, lying, cheating, and enjoying freedom by violating social laws and manners. It empowers them to stand up against injustice and make choices that promote the well-being of themselves and others. In a rapidly changing world, ethical education equips children with the skills and resilience needed to face complex moral dilemmas they may encounter in their personal, professional, and social lives.

But unfortunately, this section is more or less under the grip of commoditization. From LKG to any professional course, it can be seen that this marketing trend channelizes the students in their profiteering ways. Primarily their motive is not the well-being of the children and thereby laying the foundation of a developed country, but their aim is making a profit from it. Some English medium corporate schools receive high donations by enchanting them showing high-level infrastructure. The egotist parent falls into their trap. Most of these institutions follow a spoon-feeding system to teach to ensure a hundred percent victory. At the same time, in almost all these institutions, the tutors are not qualified properly and are also low-paid. As they are not properly trained ,their punishment method may also not be in order. Perhaps this practice may be continued almost until their admission to a professional course. The entrance coaching institutions follow this way by canvassing those egotistic parents eager to get admission to medicinal courses. Though they may score high marks in their studies, their inner growth may not be proper. These competitive minds are not getting an open perspective on human life. Because, this outlook will not coincide with their profit motive and earnings. The health sector is also under its grip. These are the general phenomena seen in our society and there may be exceptions also.

So, keeping this education sector pure is essential as it forms the foundation of any nation's development and well-being. Mismanagement in this sector can lead to substandard education and low healthcare, hindering national development and impacting citizens' quality of life. By ensuring these service sectors are proper and better ,governments can promote equitable chances to education which in turn contributes to the overall progress and prosperity and avoids the creation of two types of citizens.

The govt should give prior importance in providing high infrastructure to the children from LKG onwards and their syllabus should be strictly revised to enable them to lead a successful life. As govt. schools do not provide ample facilities and people are aware of the competition in the field of education, for their existence they depend on the private sector and are exploited. The government is only interested in providing facilities for teachers and their comfort as they will respond easily. Some farsighted people enter their children for LKG in advance in schools under the management and run entrance coaching classes. It shows our social stigma penetrating the field of education.

More over, most of the people blindly think that professional courses are the only way for their children to attain a high standard of living. Some parents bring their children for counseling to get high marks. Schools and universities prioritize revenue generation over educational quality through recruitment strategies and marketing campaigns to attract students, rather than investing in teaching resources and supporting services. This commercialization of education undermines its core purpose of fostering intellectual growth and personal development.

The children are the seed of a healthy nation and ethical concepts received from the early days are laying the groundwork for a moral development in them. We know that today's children are tomorrow's citizens. They should be released from these profiteers in the educational business. There is no point in putting manure on the ears. So children should be provided with value-based education along with providing good health. Healthy well-educated citizens are the backbone of any developed nation. All other development activities need to come only after this. The following excerpt may also be read along with this. . .

"Collapsing any nation does not require the use of atomic bombs or the use of long-range missiles. It only requires lowering the quality of education and allowing cheating in the examinations by students.

the collapse of education is the collapse of the nation."

....

Happy Vijayadashami

"Vijayadashami, more commonly known as Dasara, is a major Hindu festival celebrated annually after Durga Puja and Navaratri. The festival commemorates the victory of good over evil and signifies auspiciousness and triumph. Goddess Durga is worshipped in various forms during this festival.

Vijayadashami is observed for different reasons and is celebrated in various ways across different regions. In some places, it marks the culmination of Durga Puja, honoring Goddess Durga's triumph over the demon Mahishasura to uphold and restore righteousness.

The celebration of any festival aims to impart lessons on righteous living. Navaratri is a time to dispel ignorance and manifest the divinity within us. As our divine nature emerges, our shortcomings are subdued. Invoking deities with eight hands symbolically represents harnessing eight facets of inner strength, such as the power to accommodate, tolerate, confront, discern, judge, cooperate, withdraw, and pack up.

During this time, we also undertake 'vrat' (vows) to rise early, maintain peace, refrain from speaking ill of others, and consume only satvik (pure) food prepared with devotion. By honoring these pledges, our spiritual strength grows, guiding us from ignorance toward a brighter existence.

....

The Relevance of Spirituality in Daily Life

What is meant by spiritual knowledge for a common man? In a sentence, it may be said that it is a knowledge of our soul. Then there arises a question of what the soul is. It is an immortal subtle power that resides in a person's body and is known by many words such as Soul, Consciousness, Spirit, Chaitanya, and Atma. The body and the soul are different and residing in the body, it is the soul that thinks and acts. The body is only a costume. When a person dies this energy leaves the body. That is why we call it only a body when its soul leaves. This body is to burn or to bury, but the soul is immortal. Mind, Intellect, and our culture are part of this Soul. Spiritual science is the knowledge about this Soul, The Lord of the universe, the Supreme Soul, and the universal Drama, which means what has been happening in this universe since immemorial.

As these are subtle things and invisible it is inconceivable to many. Some people think that knowledge about the soul is a blind belief. They can believe it only on scientific evidence. But where did this scientific knowledge come from? It is the knowledge discovered by some scientists using their minds and intelligence which are part of the soul by constantly observing and experimenting. Spiritual wisdom is the knowledge of self-consciousness that combines mind, intellect, and culture. Then What other proof is needed? We don't see electricity but we experience it. We know the whole universe is hidden inside a small phone chip. We are experiencing that too without seeing. What about AI? Can we see anything? Like that, we are also experiencing God, who is called, by different names such as Shiva, Allah, Jehovah, and Iswar in each religion. Today, the whole world sees God in various forms. But despite all these differences, the form of God is generally accepted as a divine light with positive qualities like peace, love, power, knowledge, etc.

In short, GOD, Who is the Generator, Operator, and Destructor is eternal. He is without a beginning or an end. Beyond the five elements of the universe, He shines in Brahmaloka, the sixth principle, as a point of light just like the soul dwelling in the middle of the forehead, but as an ocean of divine qualities and powers. This world of light, which is silent, and infinite, is called in many names like Shantidham, Paramdham, and Nirvanadham. This is the home of all souls and the Supreme Soul. Like us living souls, God does not come in the cycle of birth and death. That is why we look above to see God whenever we want. Shiva, the Lord of the eternal comes into creation only once at the end of each Kalpa to impart the knowledge of Geetha when the Dharma is violated. After reinstating dharma He will return to his abodiment in Brahmaloka and only come in the next Kalpa in the same state. This will happen continuously as a cycle of creation. If we connect our Soul with the Supreme Soul through thought waves, we can experience God and take blessings like we tune the radio to connect with the station. This is called Meditation or Raja yoga. In our daily life, if we practice this yoga, we can see God in the form of Sachidananda(sath,chith, ananda) with the eyes of the intellect.

This is why we need some spiritual knowledge to understand God clearly. It is only possible with this subtle knowledge to self-control and to control others through our mind and intelligence. We can transform this world with our mind power and good karma following the knowledge imparted by God. If everyone is content doing virtues with positive values and radiates that energy as blessings from each other, drastic changes will happen here.

Now everyone is thamopradhana since it is the final time of the Kalpa. Even the birds and animals and the five elements of the earth are polluted because of the bad karma and the impact of negative vibrations from people addicted to evil feelings and passions like lust, anger, greed, and ego which are the signs of Kaliyuga. At the time when adharma reigns supreme, the Lord is coming to earth and giving Gitanjanam to transform souls with divine qualities like peace, love, purity, power, and knowledge. When the destruction of Kali Yuga is completed, the Satya Yuga will start called heaven.

But we don't think about that as suffering and sorrows are normal for us. When people begin to lead a holy life vibrating with peace and happiness and doing good deeds, the atmosphere will be vibrated with that. It needs great effort and God has already come to earth to do His duty as it is a part of World Drama. It is subtle and confidential and can be understood by those who come in direct contact with God through meditation and lead a holy life under His instructions. Once the Kaliyuga is completed, the Satya, Treta, and Dwapara Yugas will reach again as in order. The Wheel of Time will continue to rotate like this.

Everyone knows that if we do good, good things will happen to us. That means our destiny is in our hands and if we lead a Holi life as God's will, all issues today can be overcome. We can also extend the length of our fortune line to the future. But these are all subtle things. There lies the relevance of spiritual knowledge. Let's see how this spiritual wisdom can be applied in daily life.

First of all, we should observe pancha suddhi in our life. That means our mind, body, words, food, and karma are to be cleared. An evil thought itself is considered bad karma. It is said that we have to think twice before thinking about anything. Another thing is about food. There is a saying that, 'Like food like mind'. We know why the prasadam from the temple is important. It is because it is high-energy food vibrated with mantras. The food and water absorb vibrations easily. So when we prepare food with care and love with a pure mind and body in memory of God, it will become prasadam, a pure high-energy food. Nowadays everyone is eating by purchasing food from the store. How many people's thoughts may be absorbed in that food? The consumption of such food is likely to develop a business mentality and profit motive. we should cook food in our homes with love and care as prasadam, then naturally we will be happy and peaceful by eating that food. Each home should be kept as pure as a temple with positive vibrations and spread around. In this positive atmosphere the five principles, birds, animals trees, and plants will also be pure and calm. There will be abundance everywhere. It means that only when we change, our atmosphere will change. But now everybody looks outward and tries to change others to create peace.

The real happiness is not in things we achieve but in our minds. So we should try to look inward which needs great effort. We have to practice meditation, Raja yoga(connecting soul to super soul), or anything like that. Heaven is very near to us. If we all try together it will reach fast. We can create our destiny as well as our Heaven.

....

Happy Diwali

Diwali is a festival of lights. The lighting of lamps, candles, and bursting of crackers are part of our celebrations. It is a festival of the victory of good over evil and burn Ravanan the symbol of evil. Diwali is a time of newness. we start cleaning every nook and corner of our home and decorate it several days before. We celebrate it by giving gifts, sharing sweets, and blessing each other. But these celebrations are only superficial or external and no cleaning or newness is not happen to our inside. It is a time to start a new beginning to brighten our inner power.

Diwali is a festival of lights, symbolizing the victory of good over evil and the burning of Ravana, the embodiment of evil. As Diwali is a time of renewal, we renew our homes and surroundings and share gifts. However, these external celebrations, though joyous, often overshadow the need for inner cleansing and renewal

In other words, Diwali is not a festival for celebrating outside, it should be a celebration in our inmost heart. Nowadays we are focusing only on the outside. But we must focus on the inside as our thoughts create our actions and thus determine our destinies.

In essence, Diwali should not merely be an external celebration but a reflection of inner joy and purity. Nowadays, we tend to focus solely on outward rituals, neglecting the importance of inner reflection. Yet, the true celebration of Diwali begins within ourselves. By awakening our inner powers during Navaratri, we can extinguish the negativity symbolized by 'Ravana' within our minds. Only then can Diwali truly illuminate our hearts and surroundings.

To radiate our inner strength, we must first settle our past karmic debts and cleanse every corner of our minds with divinity and purity. We should release all past grievances and forgive ourselves and others for any wrongs. Every negative thought leaves a stain on the mind, while positive thoughts cleanse it. This inner purification allows our soul's natural power to emerge, burning away the 'Ravana' within us and illuminating our soul's power.

Meditation in the morning can help in this mental cleansing process. Spend the next few days engaging in self-reflection and positive self-talk to purify our mind. When we rid ourselves of inner stains, our soul's power shines brightly.

Remember, Diwali is not just an external celebration but an internal one. Wishing you all a joyous and meaningful Diwali.

....

Health Insurance for the Retirees-A Review

What is meant by a pension given by the government to a retired person? It is a financial assistance from the government at the time of retirement of an employee who had already spent the entire healthy period of his life serving them. It is a blessing for everyone. However, the method of determining the eligibility to receive this pension is worth thinking about.

Typically, by the time any employee has worked for about twenty-five to thirty years, they will have almost reached living standards based on their earnings. But after retirement, they should spend their life without any work and earnings. Therefore, they need assistance like pensionary benefits as a provision anyway.

At present pension is decided based on the total period of service and the salary they earned. That's where a consideration is needed. In fact, after retirement, everyone is almost the same completing their responsibilities in life and have to meet their own expenditures only. Then should the pension be granted based on the salary during their working period for the life long ? Now high-salary earners get correspondingly high pensions. Pensions of some such who cannot even go to the treasury to buy it are seen received and used by their highly-earned dependents like officials. Because the dependents of those with high salaries and circumstances are likely to reach the same level already, this money they receive without doing any work is mostly used for luxuries. Today some pensioners of this level are seen on international tours etc. If the partner is also a pensioner, their luxury is double. But that is not the case with low-paid pensioners. It is for their necessities of life and should be protected according to their earnings.

In any case, there is likely not much difference in the remaining living expenses whether he is an IAS officer or a peon who retires. So instead of paying a big amount of pension, isn't it enough to allow them to mandate free insurance with certain limits for treatment due to the likelihood of ill health by the time of retirement? Present laws and limitations in these matters are seen as inadequate.

As the standard of living of high-salary earners will also be high, those who were high officials who had rendered good service can't be honored by providing free medical insurance according to the salary they had earned. Then there will be no unnecessary expenditure or misuse of this assistance and the benefit will be available to the pensioners themselves for their treatments etc. Because nowadays the cost of treatment is comparatively high. Shouldn't the government set a limit on the basic salary to consider pension, just as the basic salary is limited to consider bonus?

Similarly, some commission members who are now receiving pensions can go to other jobs where they can later get pensions and salaries. The possibility of this double pension should also be discontinued. Nowadays it is like a saying in Malayalam that 'the elephant of 'Thevar' and wood in the jungle!" If these irregularities and disparities were rectified, how much would the government's spending be reduced?"

But what do you see today? It seems that today the laws that the British followed in the past are still prevailing. Manusmriti is a guideline for living since Vedic times. It may need to make changes over time. But some burn it and show their brilliance. But no one pays attention to the many outdated laws such as these threadbare service laws.

It is very difficult to determine how to calculate pensions, salaries, travel allowances, etc. Introducing a system such as a pay and allowances slab for each period of service based on merit and responsibility would significantly reduce the government's workload. Isn't it money that we get, no matter how it is calculated and what you call it? In any case, it is the government's responsibility to protect not only the retired government employees but the entire people.

It had regularly been seen in the media that a good part of the income is only for paying salaries and pensions to government officials. No one will object because the beneficiaries of this are those who are in power. The poor public does not know this. what can be done even if they know? Do not forget that all the people, except for a small percentage of government employees, work here though not for the government all their lives and live in this country without any allowances like old age pension, etc.

....

Dr. Renuka. KP

Sivarathri-Myth and Essence

When we look all around us what we see is sorrow, pain, worry, hatred, and lust everywhere and we think of them as normal as we have reached at the peak of kaliyuga. Does it remain so always?

God has promised in Bhagavath Geetha that whenever there is a steep decline in dharma in this world, I will descend into this world to establish it. All of us had depleted from our original nature of peace In Kaliyuga. Lust, attachment, anger, impurity, greed, jealousy, hatred, etc. became our nature and gradually became our Zanskar. As our Zanskar, the world has also changed. So, nowadays the world is passing through a darkness of unrest and ignorance. But it is true that after every night, morning has to be dawn. Just like it, after Kaliyuga Suvarnayuga has to come. But how will it happen?

We are all souls residing in this body and are away from dharma now. Dharma means to have the original qualities of the soul such as purity, power, love, peace, etc. To establish Suvarna Yuga, we have to establish dharma in our Zanskar. How it will created at this time of midnight? Now from the soul world, the Supreme Soul descends into the world during this night or in the phase of darkness of ignorance. That is why we call this day as Sivaratri.

The Supreme Soul comes into the world and explains every drop of knowledge to the soul. This drop and drop of the spiritual knowledge given by God is shown as kalasa beyond Siva linga. As drops of spiritual knowledge start falling on our intellect, intellect starts to become pure, and also we start awakening from our ignorance. The first drop of intellect that falls on us is I am not the body, qualification, position, wealth, relationship, etc. They are all Mine. I am the Soul or an Energy that drives and manages all aspects of life. The second drop was knowledge of the present time. This kaliyuga has to be transferred to Satyayuga which we have to create collectively. So God descended from the soul world to earth to give knowledge. First it was Satyayuga(golden age), then came threthayuga,dwaparayuga,andkaliyuga kaliyuga.

The soul travels through all these world circles in every Kalpa just like we move from morning to noon, to evening, and to night. As we refresh every morning after night by washing our face, the soul has to refresh in the world cycle after kaliyuga. As Satyayuga Zanskar of soul depleted in the transformation to the iron age known as kaliyuga God comes to awaken us from the deep ignorance of the soul by teaching us that I am a pure soul, peace is my original Zanskar. Power, love, knowledge, and bliss are our original nature and thus we began to wake up from ignorance. That is why Jagran (staying awakened) throughout the night. God is giving spiritual study through godly students throughout the world to create a golden age giving soul consciousness to all. When we remember God always, we are filled with divine qualities like peace ,happiness and knowledge. When all of us change our Zanskar, our sansar will be changed and the golden age will be established. This is the essence of Jagran and upavas of Sivarathri.

....

The Need of Self-transformation Today

What do we see all around us today? If we take a look at our media every day, what do we see? If we go through in between the pages of our newspapers from the first to the last in any day, it can be seen only full of negative information. All Media are competing with each other to spread this negativity. Some people who want peace in their lives are avoiding these media which from the morning when open our eyes spread negative feelings. Everyone is very much concerned about everything they see in front of them and shares complaints and worries. A lot of discussions are done in channels about every issue here and motivational speeches by spiritual scholars are carried on in their way on the other side. But there is no fruitful changes have been seen yet. It is like making noise by saying shut up.

Most of the common people are seen as addicted to these negative atmospheres and think that this is normal. Poverty, injustice, disparities, harassment, corruption, religious or political agitations, and all kinds of devaluations found in our society seem to be normal to them. Everyone thinks that life is a mixture of joys and sorrows. So when even if they are in joy, they are expecting sorrow to come to them next. That is even the happy moments are not been enjoying by them. Is there any way to release from this world of sorrows?

There is no one to find a solution for it. Why people are searching for peace? Because in their mind there is a comfort zone filled with peace that had been enjoyed by them earlier. We have to find that peace. There is only one solution to all the devaluations seen in today's society, just to change all the existing ways of thinking and think about ourselves first. If we continue to think and say in the same way as before, won't the experiences be the same as yesterday? Self-transformation is the only solution to all these problems.

Transformation of the world through self-transformation. Here we need some spiritual awareness. How much less cost! Be it political parties or social workers, they are only roaming around in their line of thought. But our intellectuals get upset when they hear about spiritual science. They want everything scientific. They don't know that spiritual science is the study of the soul which includes the mind, intellect, and culture from which these scientific thoughts are coming.

Let us watch ourselves as a witness from morning to evening. How many harmless lies each one of us are thinking, saying and doing?

Hadn't we seen ever such a father who hid in the home, telling his children to lie to those who asked about him that he was not here? He is lying to himself and training his children to lie. We all know that God is the truth. If each of us starts living with values and being truthful to ourselves, won't this place be Heaven? Purity and Truth have the Divine Power to vibrate peace and calm everywhere. With those vibrations from us, the five elements of nature will also be calm. The birds and animals are also will become calm. The atmosphere will become pure. Haven't you ever seen stray dogs running around and biting for no reason? Emotional pollution which plays a major role in making our earth hell, has become a serious problem that no one notices as it is invisible. We know that God is Sathyam, Shivam, and Sundaram. By whatever names God is called, it is Truth. If we follow the truth in our lives, will we not be Godlike? Why are we wandering for peace and happiness, by spending a lot of time and energy? If we all decide to leave the negative feelings like Kama, krodham, etc. from our lives and lead a life based on Dharma, then we need not go on a pilgrimage all over the world in search of God. Without thinking and doing this, the man wanders around seeking inner peace. It is only just enough to look back at ourselves. But no one has taught us this way of self-transformation.

None of us belong to anyone in this world. We have a parent just to get a human birth in the world. It is to be remembered that we all come to this world of theatre alone just to act a role as per the result of our karma. It is also to be remembered the naked truth that we have to go back from this theatre after the drama is over. If we understand that every moment is the final moment, then all the selfishness and grudges among the human being will automatically vanish. Is our life like that?

As a computer system has two parts software and hardware, the human being has also two parts. Our body and all things related to it are the 'Hardware' whereas 'Software' includes the mind and intellect which are commonly known as Soul or Consciousness. Unfortunately, all of us are merely body-conscious now and are trying to solve the problems related to our bodies only. When we realize we are souls, all the problems will disappear. The spiritual awareness to empower our mind and body is the only solution for all the issues and thus to maintain peace. All other knowledges are incomplete like the blind gets when he sees the elephant.

Promoting universal peace begins with encouraging personal transformation. Embrace empathy, practice kindness and cultivate a mindset of understanding. Strive for self-awareness and continue learning to contribute positively to the world. We must learn to look within ourselves instead of searching outside for peace and happiness and actually, it is the time to recognize the need for Self-Transformation for Universal Transformation.

....

The Greatest Wealth is Health. How is it to be maintained?

"To get rich, never risk your health. For it is the truth that health is the wealth of wealth."

As all we know, healthy well-educated citizens are the main asset of any nation. A better basic education and the availability of good medical facilities play crucial roles in creating powerful citizens for a developed country. Because health is the fundamental component of human capital. Investing in the health of citizens through access to healthcare, nutritious food, clean water, sanitation, and education about healthy lifestyles enhances the overall human capital of a nation. This, in turn, fosters innovation, creativity, and competitiveness on the global stage.

Healthy citizens are more productive in the workforce. They have higher energy levels, reduced absenteeism due to illness, and are generally more capable of contributing effectively to the economy. This productivity is a key driver of economic growth and prosperity. A population with good health tends to incur lower healthcare costs. Preventive measures and healthy lifestyles can help reduce the incidence of chronic diseases and the need for expensive medical interventions. Nations with robust healthcare systems and healthy populations are better equipped to respond to pandemics, natural disasters, and economic downturns. Good health enhances resilience and the ability to bounce back from adversity, ensuring continuity and stability in facing challenges. A healthy lifestyle fosters discipline, resilience, and self-control, all essential for moral development. The importance of good health among citizens cannot be overstated when constructing a developed nation.

Citizens who are healthy experience less pain, suffering, and disability, leading to overall greater well-being and happiness. This contributes to social stability and cohesion within a nation. A population with good health tends to live longer. Good health enables children to regulate emotions, make responsible decisions, and empathize with others.

So, Access to good health should be a basic human right. This fosters social justice, reduces inequality, and promotes inclusivity within society. Thus good health among citizens is paramount in constructing a developed nation. Therefore, investing in healthcare infrastructure, promoting healthy behaviors, and addressing health inequalities are critical components of nation-building efforts.

Today we have many super specialty hospitals eminent doctors and modern facilities. Though we are fortunate, the poor people can not attain them. The government provides them with medical services which are very inadequate. Even so, recently some changes have been seen in govt services by providing better facilities due to the effective intervention of social media, etc. So, good health should be a basic human right. As we said earlier, good health among citizens is paramount in constructing a developed nation. Therefore, investing in healthcare infrastructure, promoting healthy behaviors, and addressing health inequalities are critical components of nation-building efforts.

But, unfortunately, in contemporary society, the interference of business principles in sectors like health and education has become increasingly prevalent. While efficiency and profitability are often touted as benefits, their ramifications on social life are concerning. This essay explores the negative impact of a business mindset on health in social life, delving into issues such as commodification in this sector, inequality, and the erosion of communal values.

One of the primary drawbacks of applying a business mindset to the health sector is the commodification of essential services. When profit becomes the primary motive, health care is transformed from fundamental rights into market commodities.

In the health sector, the commercialization of services often leads to profitable treatments over preventive care and public health initiatives. Pharmaceutical companies may focus on developing medications for lucrative conditions rather than addressing widespread health concerns. This leads to a healthcare system that neglects the most vulnerable members of society and perpetuates disparities in health outcomes. The unethical relationship between the doctors and pharmaceutical companies may lead to ill-treatment of the patients and insist on treatment which requires complex technology in modern medicine. Why don't they promote holistic treatment by combining all types of treatments? some treatments that are unavailable in allopathy are seen in other modes of treatment like homeopathy and Ayurveda etc. and vice versa. Recently it was heard that death rate is not reduced considerably by cardiac treatment like angioplasty or angiogram.

When these treatments are used combined, aren't there any chances for patients to benefit? Eg, let us take dialysis patients, it is said that it is always not a permanent remedy. Why not recommend other treatments before getting worse and leading to transplantation or some other complex methods like dialysis? This is just a common man's suspicion. Its potentials need to be studied. Some are eager for this kind of treatment even for poor patients and support them in gathering financial assistance. considering the patient's background also, the possibility of a holistic treatment is to be examined. Modern treatment is not a watertight compartment. We must utilize all the technologies in modern medicine to find out the disease and check if we can adopt simple methods for healing in other forms of treatment.

Nowadays it is seen that almost all people are under the grip of lifestyle deceases.How did it happen? When one medicine is used for any disease it may become harmful for any other illness. Continuous medication is needed for almost all diseases like sugar ,pressure, cardiac problems, etc. Medication has become our habit today. Is there any permanent solution for this? Here lies the importance of holistic treatment of different forms.

The number of hospitals is increasing daily which means we are 'creating' the situation and we are benefitting that situation by creating job opportunities. They are promoting medical education for their benefit and students are craving to become doctors without knowing the low remuneration in private sector, especially in the dental section. Does anybody think they are all eager to do social work to serve the patient? Then why do they show reluctance to go for rural service? Their main attraction may be their high earnings and the so-called social status generated by our society. Otherwise how many other opportunities are there before them to serve the society if they desire? The health department has become one of the most profitable business areas. We made the situation so. It can be seen that most of the organizations start schools and hospitals for their charitable work. Then why do they receive donations for admission and appointments in their institutions? We have to think about all these and those who say that these education and health sectors are under the grip of commercialization can not be said as wrong.

In conclusion, it may be said that the negative impact of a business mindset in the health sector on social life is profound and far-reaching. The devaluation seen among the youth and the widespread lifestyle diseases are some of the major issues prevailing here due to the marketization of this section which need our attention and rectification. We must maintain the health sector as purely a service sector by saving the people from the magical circle of a hollow sense of pride. Can we imagine what will happen to us, if all the agriculturalists go on strike as long as any substitute for our hunger is not available in the market? All professions are important. Our approach to medical education also needs to change, then only the corruption and illegal activities in this field can be reduced.

....

The Social Media

Social media has profoundly transformed our lives, making world news and knowledge instantly accessible at our fingertips. It provides an unparalleled platform for sharing ideas and group discussions. However, social media also has its drawbacks, such as spreading misinformation, misleading people, and consuming a lot of valuable time for no purpose.

I hadn't been using social media for a very long, and initially, I encountered misinformation. I was initially amazed by the videos shared on social media, unaware of their underlying motivations. People seemed remarkably generous in sharing secrets and knowledge that seemed exclusive. For instance, once I heard a Hindu priest speak eloquently about Hindu rituals and their future consequences, it was a miracle for me, and admire our society's changing virtues. They were revealing such miraculous things that were kept so secret by some limited people like priests until then. I wondered whether concepts like Rama Rajya, Paradise, Maveli's land, or Satya Yuga have come here!

This first admiration soon gave way to a clear understanding. I realized that such sharing often had financial motives tied to viewer counts. It was a lesson in discernment — to sift through the vast knowledge offered by social media and choose what aligns with our values and needs. Some people imitate this without knowing its possibility.

Similarly, today social media has paved the way for sharing personal and confidential matters like pregnancy delivery, etc. by announcing and celebrating with families and some celebrities sharing such moments wisely to obtain high reach to their shows. These posts aren't merely personal but also to attract audiences seeking engagement. It's quite different from earlier days when singers and actors gathered attention through their talent, captivating audiences from all walks of life.

How fortunate were the singers and actors who were thought to be unique in the past? We thought that they had no alternates here. But social media demolished that fact through the songs and acting of all ages, from children to housewives and whole families. It may also seen that some crooked youth by overcoming our traditions and customs marry fair girls and try to earn money by showcasing their personal lives on social media. Perhaps, this is merely a sign of changing times.

Nevertheless, living in the age of social media brings its blessings. Whether it's seeking medical advice, learning new tricks, or exploring spiritual mantras, everything is at our fingertips. With a click, we can get all the information about the universe. The key to happiness lies in choosing what to study, what to listen to, and what to watch. However, it's also evident that negative news spreads like wildfire, showing how much excitement this negative news stirs among the audience. Sadly, much attention is often given to matters deemed more sensitive than important to our lives. Monetization should not be done based on the number of viewers. There must have some other filtering is also needed. Although social media has changed our lives beyond what we could have dreamed of, its role in generating emotional turmoil is increasing daily and cannot be ignored.

....

Dr. Renuka. KP

It is Just a Dream

I had a wonderful dream yesterday. There is nothing to fear, but there is also a bit of humor in it... What may be the reason? Let me tell you.

I am a social worker, I don't have any special job. But I am not a full-time politician. I have no difficulty doing this social work because I have a modest financial position in our family. Moreover, I am a member of many social organizations in our locality. I reach any places where the hills are cut down and level illegally or the land is filled unknowingly. Anyway, I am an integral part of the Panchayat. Today was also something special to us as our organization bought and donated an ambulance to the hospital in our panchayat. With great satisfaction of being part of a good deed, I went to bed and quickly fell asleep.

Then an angel form appeared in front of him dressed in a garment of light. What a brilliance it was! The figure came near me and called me. I was stunned. A light as we see in movies. I tried to jump out of bed but in vain.

'Don't be afraid. I have come to help you. You have been suffering for the sake of the natives for a long time.'

'Yes', I said with some elegance. 'I like this kind of social service.' I continued.

'What are you doing all this for?'

"I am doing all this for the good of the natives."

'What did you do for them?'

"I tried to bring a hospital to our panchayath. Now I have also brought an ambulance. There was no police station in this village. Now, as a result of my efforts, the police station has started. Now we want to have a civil court as well."

'Does the number of hospitals, police stations, or courts represent the measurement of the development of your society ?'

"Until now, we had to go to other nearby cities for treatment.' I said confidently.

'You are struggling to establish a police station, court hospitals, etc. Students, trying to become doctors, advocates, policemen, etc at any cost. Don't you know that all these are needed at the time of a decline in the virtues of our nation? We do not need all of these. Why don't you dream of a land without patients or criminals, where everyone is healthy, happy, pure, and contented in abundance?' Then the angel asked me.

"Oh, how can that happen? Isn't it like this in every country?'I asked in suspicion.

'Bro, you have misunderstood that this is the world, and all the evils are thought to be normal. You deserve to live in a world full of peace and happiness without any poverty, diseases, and criminals. This is what you call Heaven. You were in Heaven. That is why you are all seeking comfort in peace and happiness'. Angel said.

Then I said, "Oh, I can't even think like that."

'That's what we need to work for. A land where there is no need for a stethoscope, no screaming sound of an ambulance, no stretcher, no wheelchair, no doctors, no criminals, and no lawyers in black coats advocating for justice! A prosperous land with a peaceful nature without any calamities. That is what is meant by progress. May you and your country escape from this degradation.' that angel told him.

You are talking a lot about the law of attraction. In this degenerate, dirty world, doctors are waiting to get the sick and the advocates are expecting injustice. If the law of attraction works as you say, what may be the result?

"Why are you scaring me, what can I do even if it is so?"

'Everyone thinks like that. That is the reason why this land is so. Realize your history and geography and your spiritual strength. You were the souls existing here at the time of Sanathana Devi Devatha Sanskar. while continuing several rebirths, you forgot yourselves. This is all happening here, as per in the world drama in every Kalpa. Now it is the time to realize and regain powers by bringing purity in your thoughts and deeds. You are the souls, the children of Almighty Supreme Soul. Realize yourself and use your spiritual power in life.'

Hearing the words of the angel, I got bored. But I could not say a word. I could not even stand up from there. Then angel continued.,

'If you change into Devi Devatha Sanskar, then your family will begin to change and thereby your neighbors. That way, the whole nation. Let it start from you. Awaken the sleeping energy in you. Bring truth, dharma, and purity into your life. Then you can see that your soul power is awakened.'

"Are all these true?"I asked.

'For long, you have been knocking on every door for happiness and peace. You go for the pilgrimage in search of peace and god's grace. By stopping this, change your sanskar. Instead of begging god, try to become like a god by bringing divine qualities. Manasa vacha, karmana, be truthful to ourselves and the world. A golden age is waiting for you. A heavenly kingdom with rich golden palaces, where deers and lions flow with honey and milk and drink from the same pond. People, birds, and animals are living peacefully and happily. You take the initiative and achieve it yourself.'

When I heard so much, I felt sad. As if I didn't understand anything. I felt like drinking some water. When somehow I dared to jump out of bed, I lost my dream and the Angel disappeared.

'Was this a dream or reality? I have heard that God is Light as per any Dharma here.. Is it God who came into my dream? Is this something that will happen? 'All confusion.

I stood up from there and took some water from the jug. After drinking, he pulled the blanket again and started to sleep. When It was morning he told everyone in the home about the dream. No one believed him. 'This is a dream not for intending others. It is for me to be transformed.' I consoled myself.

....

The Angels on Earth

I am retelling the story of the train journey. After leaving the train station from Kozhikode to Tirur, a boy sitting on the opposite side of me started vomiting. Their mother and two children were alone on their journey. It seems that I have to get off at the next station. There was not much luggage. I felt bad for the child when I heard him vomiting, but I got up from there and moved to the other seat. The fellow passenger who was talking to me was sitting there and watching what happened. It is difficult for me to see all this. The mental strength is not enough. The mother of the child tried to comfort him by rubbing him and so on. They are trying. The elder boy is looking at him helplessly. There is a lot of panic on their faces. Everyone on the train is looking at the boy but no one is doing anything.

When I was helplessly sitting like that, a young girl got up from the next room after hearing the noise. The girl brought a plastic envelope from her bag and sat beside the child caring for him. She sit for a while there listening to him. In any case, there was a small relief for the moment. The child's mother also felt a great peace. It was only later that I realized that the girl was a nursing student. When many people tried to move away, I felt respect for that girl who came close and lovingly comforted her. That was the first time I felt how true it is to say that nurses are angels on earth. That girl showed me that if we let go of some people who work only as a way of earning for living, then they are the angels on earth. I prayed with my heart that the girl should have all the good things. Having seen the misbehavior of nurses in government hospitals, I didn't think it was appropriate to call them angels.s. But when we remember some health workers who succumbed to death after treating Corona patients, we can't help bowing our heads in front of them.

....

About the Author

Dr. Renuka. KP

Mrs. Renuka K.P. a retired Tahsildar is a native of Ernakulam district in Kerala. She is a content writer and also a Youtuber. She has published two story books in English and one in Malayalam. She has also written stories in some anthologies and received several recognitions including international awards for her literary works. WCEPC has awarded her an Honorary Doctorate in Literature with their membership.

Her stories have been translated into five foreign languages.